MR PLOD AND THE TRAIN ROBBERS

This edition first published in Great Britain by HarperCollins Publishers Ltd in 1999

1 3 5 7 9 10 8 6 4 2

ISBN: 0 00 1361600

Cover design and illustrations by County Studio
A CIP catalogue for this title is available from the British Library.
The HarperCollins website address is:
www.fireandwater.com

Printed and bound in Great Britain

MR PLOD AND THE TRAIN ROBBERS

Collins

An Imprint of HarperCollins*Publishers*

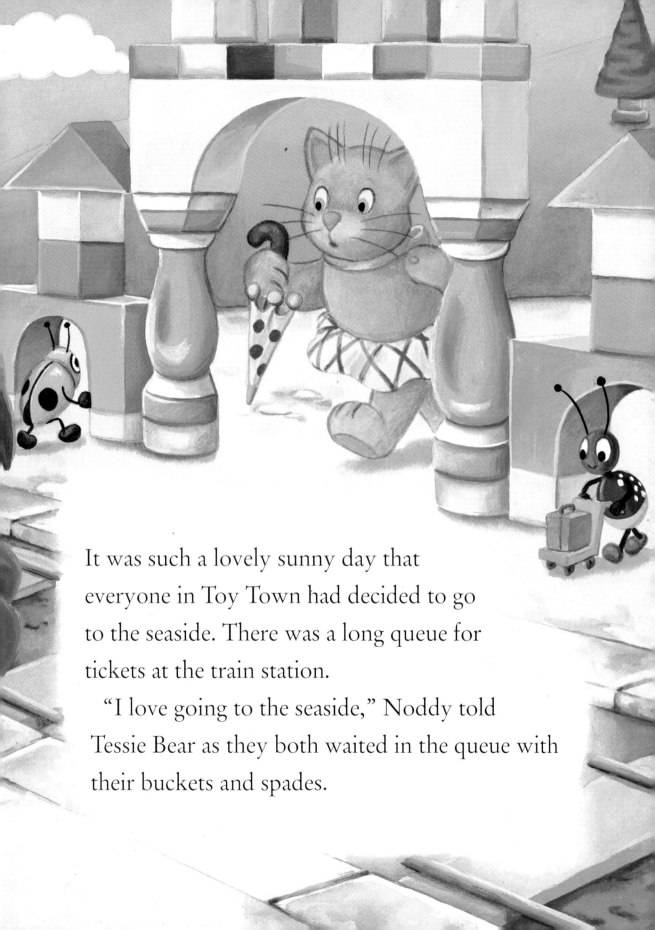

It was such a lovely sunny day that everyone in Toy Town had decided to go to the seaside. There was a long queue for tickets at the train station.

"I love going to the seaside," Noddy told Tessie Bear as they both waited in the queue with their buckets and spades.

The goblins were the only ones who weren't going to the seaside. They didn't have enough money to buy a train ticket. They watched jealously from behind a tree.

"I wish we were going to the seaside and eating ice-creams all day," said Sly.

"Me too," said Gobbo. "It's just not fair!"

Mr Plod joined the queue for tickets.

"Hello, Mr Plod!" said Noddy. "Are you going to the seaside, too?"

"Yes, young Noddy," replied Mr Plod, huffing a bit because the queue was so long.

"But you've forgotten your bucket and spade!" said Noddy.

"Bucket and spade!" snorted Mr Plod.
"A policeman doesn't have time for buckets and
spades. I'm going to the seaside on very important
business!"

Mr Plod then explained how he was taking two special bracelets to the seaside with him. They had been stolen from Mrs Feather Hat, who was the mayor at the seaside. Fortunately, Mr Plod had caught the robber and he was now taking the bracelets safely back to Mrs Feather Hat.

"These bracelets have to be guarded with my life!"
Mr Plod added, puffing out his chest sternly.
"They are made of solid gold and worth a great
deal of money!"

From behind the tree, the two goblins gasped.

"Did you hear that, Gobbo?" Sly exclaimed.

"Yes I did!" Gobbo replied. "Are you thinking what I am thinking, Sly?"

Sly certainly *was* thinking what Gobbo was thinking!

The two goblins raced off to the Dark Wood. They planned to hide in the tunnel that the train was going to have to pass through on its way to the seaside. They were going to block the tunnel so that the train would get stuck and they could climb on board in the darkness and steal the bracelets from Mr Plod's pocket!

The goblins had plenty of time to get everything ready for their wicked plan. The queue at the station was so long that the train wasn't able to leave for another half an hour.

"Please take your seats everyone!" the driver called anxiously from the engine. "We're running late enough as it is."

Noddy excitedly squeezed in next to Tessie Bear, putting his bucket and spade on his knee.

Everyone on the train was excited. Everyone, that
is, except Mr Plod. He sat all on his own in the
carriage right at the back of the train. He had a
grim look on his face: it was a big responsibility
keeping hold of those valuable bracelets!

At last the train started to move. **CLANK! CLANK! CLANK!** "Hooray!" shouted Noddy as the train went faster and faster.

Soon it was going at full speed, and the driver was blowing his whistle.

Toot, Toot! Toot, Toot!

The train rushed past the houses, then it entered the Dark Wood.

"We're coming to the tunnel!" Noddy cried, turning to Tessie excitedly. "I love going through tunnels!"

Suddenly, everything went dark, and all the passengers had to hold on to their hats as the wind rushed into their faces. Their voices echoed loudly. But then…

SCR-E-E-E-E-E-CH!

Noddy and Tessie grabbed hold of each other as they were nearly thrown out of their seats. The train had stopped suddenly in the middle of the tunnel.

"Sorry everyone!" the train driver shouted anxiously in the darkness. "There's a big tree across the line at the exit to the tunnel."

While the train driver got out to look at the tree, the
goblins, who had been hiding behind the train, tiptoed
to the carriage in which Mr Plod was sitting. Then,
very gently, Gobbo put his hand into Mr Plod's
pocket, feeling for the bracelets.

"Got one!" he whispered, slipping the bracelet over his wrist.

"And I've got the other!" Sly exclaimed, doing exactly the same with the second bracelet.

Mr Plod suddenly heard them.

"Here…what's going on?" he cried.

But the goblins had already run out into the
tunnel. However, as they skipped over the fallen
tree, they both suddenly fell to the ground at the
same time.

"How did that happen?" cried Sly as he rubbed his head.

"*That* happened," Mr Plod chuckled as he hurried up to them, "because you slipped your wrists into my handcuffs by mistake! The gold bracelets were in my *other* pocket!"

Anyway, it wasn't long before everyone had helped the train driver move the tree off the line, and the train was able to continue its journey.

Noddy, Tessie, Master Tubby and their friends had a great day at the seaside.

The goblins spent the day away from home as well. But not at the seaside…not in the sunshine…

…*In Mr Plod's prison!*

Join the Noddy in Toyland Club

- **Birthday Card**
- **Christmas Card**
- **News and Offers**
- **Welcome Pack**
  including a super video phone

When you become a member of the fantastic Noddy in Toyland Club you'll receive a personal letter from Noddy, a club badge, and a superb Welcome Pack of Toyland fun – including the fully featured Noddy video phone, sticker scene with re-useable stickers, activity poster and more!

You'll also get birthday and Christmas cards from Noddy and his friends, plus news and offers from Toyland.

A year's membership is just **£9.99** (plus 93p postage). It's guaranteed superb value – if you are not delighted simply return the pack within 14 days for your money back.

How to Enrol

Send the following details, together with cheque for the total amount (payable to Robell Clubs) to: The Noddy in Toyland Club PO Box 142, Horsham RH13 5FJ.

Details required: New member's full name, date of birth and address including postcode, name of child's parent or guardian at the same address, and your name address (if different to information already given). If you require a Club T-Shirt, request size from: age 3-4, 5-6, or 7-8.

Calculate total amount payable: £10.92 (inc postage) for each membership plus £5.99 for each Club T-Shirt.

To order by credit card, have the same details ready and call our customer helpline on 01403 242727 or fax 01403 261555

Data Protection Act: If not wish to receive ot offers from us or com, we recommend, pleas this on your applicatio